THIS BOOK
BELONGS TO...

Old Billy's

Enchanted Valley

Written & Illustrated by
BRUCE PEARDON
Mouth Painter

Dedicated to the memory of little Natalie Moore

Published by the Association of Mouth and Foot Painting Artists
1st Edition
©

"Nobody really remembers when Old Billy first came to the place which everyone now knows as Old Billy's Valley. It seems that one day there was no-one living in a ramshackle farmhouse which had been deserted for many years, and then suddenly, Old Billy was there, making repairs, planting trees and filling the air with his beautiful music."

A little joey kangaroo sat wide eyed as he listened to his grandfather tell the story of Old Billy's Enchanted Valley.

"But what happened to Old Billy, Grandad . . . why isn't he here anymore?"

"Now be patient, young fellow, and let me tell the story from the beginning," said Grandfather gently.

"You see, this valley has always been beautiful . . . except for a time when it was almost destroyed. My grandfather told me of how as a little joey he watched the humans with their axes and saws almost ruin it forever."

"You mean humans like Old Billy?" interrupted the joey.

"No. Not all humans are the same. Many have always cared about Nature's wonders, and many more are learning to care, because of people like Old Billy . . . Now where was I?"

"You were saying how the valley was nearly destroyed," said the joey eagerly.

"Ah yes, said Grandfather. "These humans came to farm the land . . . "

"What does that mean?" asked the joey curiously.

"It means to grow food . . . you see all the creatures on Earth need to eat, and we all get our food in different ways . . . Humans need farms to grow food . . . but," said Grandfather wearily, "that is where they make big mistakes."

"Why?" asked the joey.

"Well, as I have told you, we are all creatures on this Earth and we have to share what Nature provides, but nearly all humans take more than their share."

"How Grandad?"

Because they destroy what they think they don't need . . . but they are slowly learning that every living thing on Earth is here for a purpose and if they interfere with the wonders of Nature too much, then they will lose it all . . . that's what nearly happened in this valley."

"Until Old Billy saved it," said the joey gleefully.

"That's right! I remember my grandfather telling me how the farmers who first came here cut down nearly all the trees and burnt them."

"But where did the birds build their nests?" asked the little kangaroo anxiously.

"There was nowhere for them to build their nests, nor were there any gum leaves for the koalas or food for the possums and hundreds of other creatures that lived here. So they all disappeared."

"But what about kangaroos? Did they have to leave too?"

"Well," sighed Grandfather, "for a while the kangaroos were able to feed on the little grass that had remained undisturbed by the farmer's plough, and sleep in the shelter of the few patches of trees that still stood on the hills . . . but when no rain came, the grass was soon gone and there was nothing left to eat."

"So what did the kangaroos do, Grandad?"

"At first they tried to eat what the farmers had grown, however this made the farmers angry and they used guns to frighten the kangaroos away. So there was nothing left to do but search for food elsewhere."

"But if there was no rain, how did the humans get food?" asked the joey.

"Ah! A good question, little fellow . . . You see, getting no rain was just the start of all the problems they had caused by cutting down the trees; without birds to control the insects that damage farmers' crops, the insects just about wiped out what the farmers had planted!"

"So the insects ate the humans' food," said the joey eagerly.

"Not only insects! But mice as well . . . you see without hawks, owls and other predators to prey on the mice, they were able to breed in millions and ruined what was left of the farmers' crops."

"So then the farmers had to leave to find other food," stated the joey.

"Not right away . . . They tried to plant different crops but then they discovered other reasons why trees are so important."

"What are they, Grandad?"

"Well, little fellow . . . without the blossoms on the trees there was nothing to attract the bees and other insects that help pollinate the farmers' crops, so nothing would grow. Then worst of all, when a really bad drought struck, there were no trees to form a windbreak against the hot winds from the north, and much of the soil that the farmers had ploughed was blown away."

"As if that wasn't enough, when the rains came more of the soil was washed away because there was nothing left to hold it together."

"So that's when the farmers left?" asked the joey.

"Yes. They left to farm somewhere else and hopefully they were wise enough to learn from their mistakes."

"Maybe there shouldn't be humans on Earth, then nothing would get ruined," said the joey.

"No. As I've told you every living creature on Earth has a purpose. Humans need farms for food . . . Look around you. There are once again farms in the valley, but they don't take too much. They share with Nature. There are trees growing, birds and animals are living in them, the river is flowing and clean . . . ducks and waterfowl have returned."

"And it's all beautiful again because of Old Billy . . ." said the joey happily.

"Yes . . . he came and helped repair what others had ruined."

"Do you remember him, Grandad?"

"Oh yes! I was just a little joey like you when I first peeped out of my mother's pouch and saw Old Billy, and it was then my grandfather told me the story I'm telling you."

"And it's your story too," said the joey earnestly.

"Oh yes, some of it is my story too," chuckled Grandfather. "Now, from what I was told, there had been very dry weather, and the mob of kangaroos which my grandfather led, knew that although there was very little to eat, there was still water here in the river, and that was when they first saw Old Billy."

"What was he doing?"

"Well, at the time, he was repairing a farmhouse; it was then however your great-great grandfather and the other kangaroos noticed all the little trees planted along the river banks and they became very curious."

"What did they do?"

"Nothing. They watched him for a while, had a drink and then went off in search of food. It was soon after that good rains came and they didn't return to the valley for a long time . . . You can imagine their surprise when they did, for there were trees everywhere and lush grass, and still Old Billy was planting more little trees."

"Is that when you remember him, Grandad?"

"Yes. I remember so well how there were birds everywhere . . . kookaburras, lorikeets, galahs, butcher birds . . . the valley rang with the beautiful sound of birdcalls . . . "

"Then in the evening, when Old Billy's day's work was done, the valley would be filled with the strains of his music, as he would sit on his front verandah and play his violin or squeezebox or perhaps his tin whistle."

"What is a squeezebox and the other things you mentioned?" said the joey in a puzzled voice.

"That's something you will learn in time." said Grandfather with a twinkle in his eye.

"None of the animals were afraid of Old Billy, and when we heard his music, we would all quietly approach him so we could watch him play … Some of the birds, the galahs and the butcher birds became so bold they would perch right on Old Billy and screech and sing in time with the melody."

"And I must confess, sometimes an emu and I would entertain the throng with a merry jig," he chuckled

"You used to dance!" exclaimed the joey.

"My word I did . . . I was quite nimble on my feet as a young fellow," said Grandfather modestly.

"But you haven't told me what happened to Old Billy," said the joey anxiously.

"I'll get to that part of the story shortly," answered Grandfather smiling, "Just don't be too impatient ... Now where was I? Oh yes ... Anyway, one day, some of us noticed Old Billy opening some big boxes ... and what do you think shyly peeped out of them?"

"What?" asked the joey excitedly.

"Well! There were possums, koalas, echidnas, bandicoots and all sorts of animals ... ! They timidly greeted each other at first and then they became bolder, so they decided to investigate their new home. That's when we kangaroos went and met them. They told us they had come from a zoo which had closed down and that Old Billy had bought them so that he could set them free. So you see, the valley was changing back to how it once was."

"Except for the humans," added the joey.

"Ah yes! Don't forget, however, that there's plenty of space for everyone if it's cared for, but no place for anyone if it's not!"

"I understand," said the joey quietly.

"Now what happened was, that other humans saw what Old Billy was doing and they wanted to help. Soon there were many people planting trees and clearing the river so it would once again flow freely. All of this made Old Billy very happy, and he played his music even more sweetly. So the valley seemed filled with his enchantment."

"But why has Old Billy gone now, Grandad?"

Grandfather kangaroo spoke gently, "You see, my little one, there is part of the story that only the kangaroos know...something you must tell the little joeys when you are old..."

"What is it, Grandad? asked the joey timidly.

"My grandfather knew Old Billy... Old Billy was a little boy then... he was the son of one of the farmers who first came to this valley..."

"Those who cut down the trees?"

"That's right . . . Old Billy knew it was wrong what had happened in this beautiful place. So he came back to try and heal the land . . . But when his task was finished he was an old man, and like all creatures when they become very sick or old, Old Billy died. So his friends in the valley put him in the ground and put a stone where he lies."

HERE RESTS
OLD BILLY
A FRIEND
OF
NATURE

"The little joey thought for a moment and then said sadly, "Will you die Grandad?"

"Yes, one day, little one, all of us die when we're old . . . sometimes creatures die when they're young . . . you see, we don't really die. Our bodies may go away but all of us keep living by the memories we leave with others . . . Old Billy can never die because humans and animals will always remember how he brought this valley back to life, and they will always hear his music."

"And I'll always remember you, Grandad, because of this story," said the joey happily.

"I'm glad," smiled Grandfather.

Then the joey frowned and asked in a puzzled voice, "But, Grandad, if Old Billy is dead, how will we always hear his music?"

Grandfather gave a chuckle. "Come with me and I'll show you something . . . " and the old kangaroo led the little joey to a hollow in a tree.

"When Old Billy died the other humans just left his house the way it was. No-one seemed to want the things with which Old Billy made music. So some of his animal friends kept them.

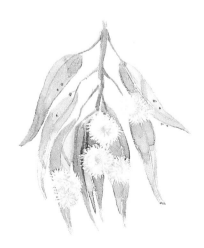

The Grandfather reached inside the tree and pulled out a bag and from it removed a violin, a squeezebox and a tin whistle. Then he raised his head and gave a whistle in the direction of a nearby patch of scrub.

Immediately, a koala and a possum climbed down from their trees and came over to the old kangaroo.

The joey watched in fascination as the trio took up the instruments. Grandfather had the violin, the koala the squeezebox and possum the whistle.

At a nod from Grandfather they began to play, at which the joey was totally spellbound. Almost immediately, birds began to flitter and dance about, and the glade was filled with happy sounds.

The lilting sound of music drifted through the valley and all the birds began to mimic its tuneful song. Thus the memory of an old man who loved the trees and the creatures of the bush, will be treasured always. For whenever a bird sings, whether it's a magpie greeting the day with its melodious warble, or the ringing call of the whipbird from its forest glade, it's telling the story of Old Billy's enchanted valley.

THE END

ANIMALS AND BIRDS OF AUSTRALIA

Grey Kangaroo, front cover, P3, 16, 21, 38, 41.
A marsupial, one of Australia's largest kangaroos, found in the forest and scrubland of Eastern Australia.

Baby kangaroo or joey p16, 33, 38.
Lives in mother's pouch until it's old enough to fend for itself.

Koala. Ownership page, p29, 41.
A tree dwelling marsupial that lives exclusively on the leaves of the eucalypt tree.

Wombat. p29.
A marsupial that lives in burrows. It is mainly nocturnal and lives on grass and herbage.

South-west Pygmy Possum. p7, 39.
Is a nocturnal marsupial that feeds on insects and the nectar of flowering trees.

Ringtail Possum. Front cover, p41.
A very common nocturnal marsupial. It has a long prehensile tail and is about the size of a domestic cat. Found widely throughout Australia. Feeds on fruit, blossoms and insects.

Echnida or Spiny anteater. p29.
A mammal that lays eggs and has long sharp spines which it protectively raises when threatened with danger. It lives on ants which it digs for with its long claws.

House Mouse. p11.
Probably originating in Asia but now widely distributed throughout the world. Reaches plague proportion in Australia and attacks cereal crops.

Galah. Front cover, p24, 41.
They are widely distributed throughout Australia. They build their nests in hollow trees and are mainly ground-feeding seed-eaters.

Rainbow Lorikeet. p38, 41.
Distributed along the coast of Australia from Cape York in Queensland to Spencer Gulf in South Australia. Nests in hollow tree limbs and feeds on seeds, berries, fruit, blossoms and insects.

Eastern Rosella. Front cover.
Found on the coastal fringe of southern Australia. Nests in a hole in a tree and relies on fruit, blossoms, seeds and insects for food.

Kookaburra or Laughing Jackass. p21.
The most familiar of Australia's birds because of its distinctive laughing call. It is the largest member of the kingfisher family. It nests in tree hollows and exists on a diet of insects, small rodents, grubs, worms and small reptiles.

Sacred Kingfisher. p31.
Found everywhere in Australia except the dry inland. Nests in termite mounds, dry banks or tree hollows. Feeds on small lizards, beetles and grubs and when located near water, (salt or fresh) will dive for fish and crustaceans.

Grey Butcherbird. p23, 41.
Found extensively in the southern half of Australia and part of the far north. One of the most beautiful songsters in the world. It is a predator and derives its name from its habit of 'butchering' its prey of small reptiles etc., by skewering it on a thorn or sharp twig and tearing it apart with its sharp bill. Builds a neat, softly lined twig nest in a tree fork about ten metres off the ground.

Magpie. p42.
Is found widely throughout Australia and like the butcherbird, has a beautiful call and preys on insects, grubs and small reptiles. It can be very bold and is often fed by householders or picnicers on scraps. Builds a twig nest high in the eucalypts.

Noisy Miner. Back cover, p20.
Found in the eastern quarter of Australia. Feeds on insects and nectar and builds a nest of loose twigs and silk from moth cocoons.

Spotted pardalote. p6, 36.
A beautiful little bird that builds its nest by burrowing into creek banks or cliff faces. It is found along the Australian east coast as well as Tasmania and the corner of West Australia. It eats moths, caterpillars, insects and spiders.

Emu. p27.
The world's second largest flightless bird. Lives in most parts of Australia. Eats seeds, blossoms and native fruit; also a variety of grass shoots, herbage and insects. Female lays her eggs on a cleared spot on the ground and then the male incubates them and rears the chicks.

Chestnut teal. p15.
Found in southern and the western corner of Australia and Tasmania. Nests in reeds or hollow trees low to the water. Feeds on seeds and water grasses.

Superb blue wren. Front cover, p35.
Found in the southern half of the eastern coast fringe of Australia and Tasmania. Builds a neat ball of grass woven and lined with spider web. Lives on insects.

"Old Billy's Enchanted Valley" is the third children's book Bruce Peardon has written and illustrated, the previous two being "Charlie the Chimneysweep and Sooty" and "Teddy's Night Lost in the Bush". Both of these have been best sellers and have been translated into five languages and sold worldwide.

As a child, Mr Peardon had always shown a keen interest in art, but it was not until at the age of seventeen, when a motor accident left him totally paralysed, that he was determined to succeed as a professional artist by painting with the brush held in his mouth.

Mr Peardon has been a member of the Mouth and Foot Painting Artists Association for twenty years, and is not only a successful illustrator, but has won acclaim for his fine art work as well, with paintings in private collections throughout the world. He is married and lives with his wife, Christine, and son, Ben, in south-east Queensland, Australia.